for Oliver

The Excavator Who Didn't Want to Dig

Copyright © 2023 by Kelly Pacheco

ISBN
979-8-9885494-2-0 (Hardcover)

979-8-9885494-0-6 (Paperback)

The Excavator
who didn't
want to
Dig

On a construction site not too far away, Digger the excavator was busily digging away at the dirt.

He was working very hard but feeling very small.
When he looked around, he felt like everyone
else's job was much bigger than his.

Dumper, the dump truck, hauled huge loads of dirt and rock, creating mountains where he dumped them.

"Hey there, Dumper! Will you teach me to carry big loads like you?"

"Sure, follow me. I'll show you what I do!"

But being a dump truck is impossible...

The excavator rolled off the construction site with a frown.

"That is the perfect job for me! A garbage
truck is what I should be!"

"Hey there, Garby! Can you teach me how to pick up trash like you?"

"Oh, I'd love to show you what I do!"

But being a garbage truck
is not much fun...

"I think this isn't the job for me," Digger
grumbled, and away he went.

But being a steamroller is not the best idea...

when
you
have
super
sharp
teeth

In the field, Digger's friend, Harvee, the combine harvester, was cutting through thick rows of wheat.

"Well, that's not the job for me," Digger
said, and away he rolled again.

When he looked up, he saw a jumbo jet swoop across the sky.

Digger returned to the construction site, surprised to find it was silent. Dumper couldn't dump if he had no load to carry. The other machines couldn't do their work without the extra dirt being hauled away.

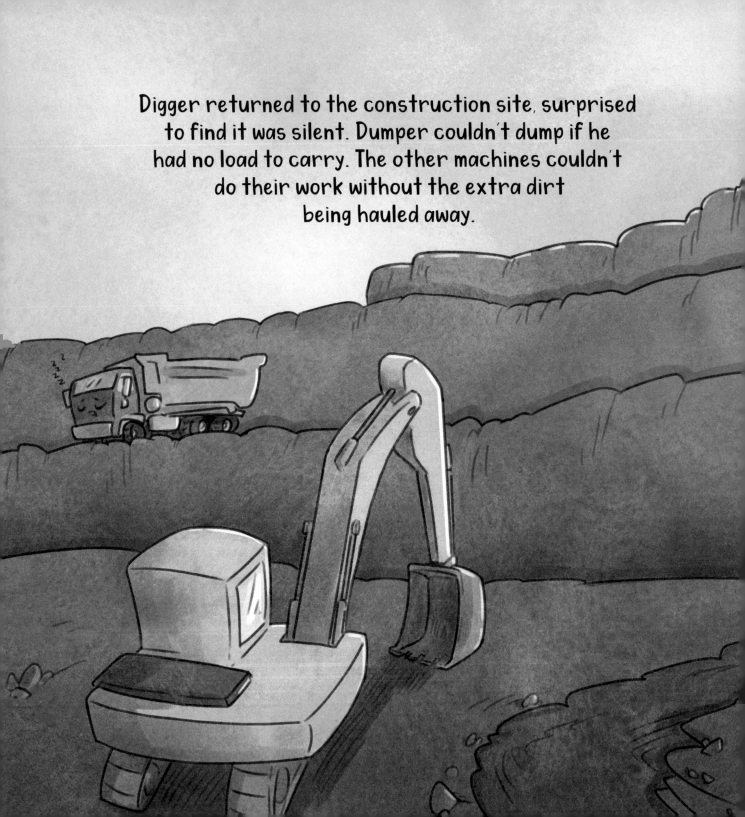

Everyone was wondering what they would do
since Digger wasn't there to dig.

Digger was amazed. He rushed to Dumper's side
and started digging right away.

The whole site seemed to come back to life
with engines rumbling all around.

Digger smiled.
"THIS is the perfect job for me.
An excavator is what I should be!"

So the next time you see an excavator busily digging at a construction site, don't forget to give a little cheer to let him know he's doing great!

A note from the author:

Here's a little shout out to all the moms, dads, teachers, and caregivers reading this book, who may feel like your place in the world is very small. Just know that you too were designed for a very specific purpose and your little footprint does, indeed, have a big impact on the world. More people than you know are depending on you and admiring you for your own strengths and abilities. So go ahead and do what you do best—we've got a lot of work to do!

God bless,
Kelly.

If you enjoyed reading this book, it would mean the world to me if you left a positive review!

Kelly is a stay-at-home mom turned first-time author who lives in Texas with her husband and two children. After struggling with feeling very small and insignificant shortly after giving birth to her second child, she decided to write a story to help her own children and others feel proud of their place in the world. When she isn't dreaming up her next story, you can find her living out her vocation as a wife and mother with a renewed sense of pride in the mundane.

Jared is an illustrator who lives in Utah with his wife and two boys. He had an excavator obsessed child and is happy to finally be doing an excavator book! You can find more of his work at Salmondjoy.artstation.com

Made in United States
Troutdale, OR
02/02/2024

17384222R10024